For my friend and illustrator
extraordinaire, Pat Schories!
—A.S.C.

HarperCollins® and I Can Read Book® are trademarks of HarperCollins Publishers.

Library of Congress Cataloging-in-Publication Data
Capucilli, Alyssa Satin, date
  Biscuit meets the class pet / by Alyssa Satin Capucilli ; illustrated by Pat Schories. — 1st ed.
    p. cm. — (My first I can read)
  Summary: When Nibbles, the class pet, gets lost during a visit, Biscuit the puppy helps find him.
  ISBN 978-0-06-117747-7 (trade bdg.) — ISBN 978-0-06-117749-1 (pbk.)
  [1. Dogs—Fiction. 2. Animals—Infancy—Fiction. 3. Rabbits—Fiction.] I. Schories, Pat, ill. II. Title.
PZ7.C179Bislm 2010   2008044032
[E]—dc22   CIP
                                                                                                                      AC

10 11 12 13 14   LP/WOR   10 9 8 7 6 5 4 3 2 1   ❖   First Edition

Biscuit Meets the Class Pet

story by ALYSSA SATIN CAPUCILLI

pictures by PAT SCHORIES

HARPER

An Imprint of HarperCollinsPublishers

Here, Biscuit.

Come meet Nibbles!

Woof, woof!

This is Nibbles.

Nibbles is our class pet.

Nibbles is here for a visit.

Woof, woof!

Hop, hop!

Look, Biscuit!

Nibbles found your bone.

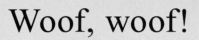

Woof, woof!

Hop, hop!
Nibbles found your ball.

Woof, woof!

Hop, hop!
Nibbles found your bed, too!

Woof!

Silly puppy!

No tugging.

Stay here, Biscuit.
I will get a snack
for Nibbles.

Woof, woof!

Hop, hop!

Woof!

Hop, hop!

Woof!
Hop, hop!

19

Woof, woof! Woof, woof!

Hop!

Oh no, Biscuit!

Where is Nibbles?

Woof, woof!

We must find him.

Woof, woof!

Nibbles is not under the table.

Woof, woof!

Nibbles is not on the chair.

Woof, woof!

Where can Nibbles be?

Woof, woof!
Sweet puppy!

Nibbles found your bone
and your ball
and your bed!

Woof, woof!
And you found Nibbles.
Woof!